Welcome
to a special
puppet show.
It is
about the Maccabees.
Who were the Maccabees?
Let's find out.

Series of Holiday Books by the Authors
LIKE A MACCABEE
The High Holy Day Do-It-Yourself Dictionary
A Purim Album
But This Night Is Different: A Seder Experience
Shabbat Can Be

To the Maccabees of every era—
may your spirit live on
Raymond A. Zwerin and Audrey Friedman Marcus

To the memory of
Leonard Eisner, a dear man
Giora Carmi

Copyright © 1991 by
The Union of American Hebrew Congregations
Manufactured in the United States of America
10 9 8 7 6 5 4 3 2 1

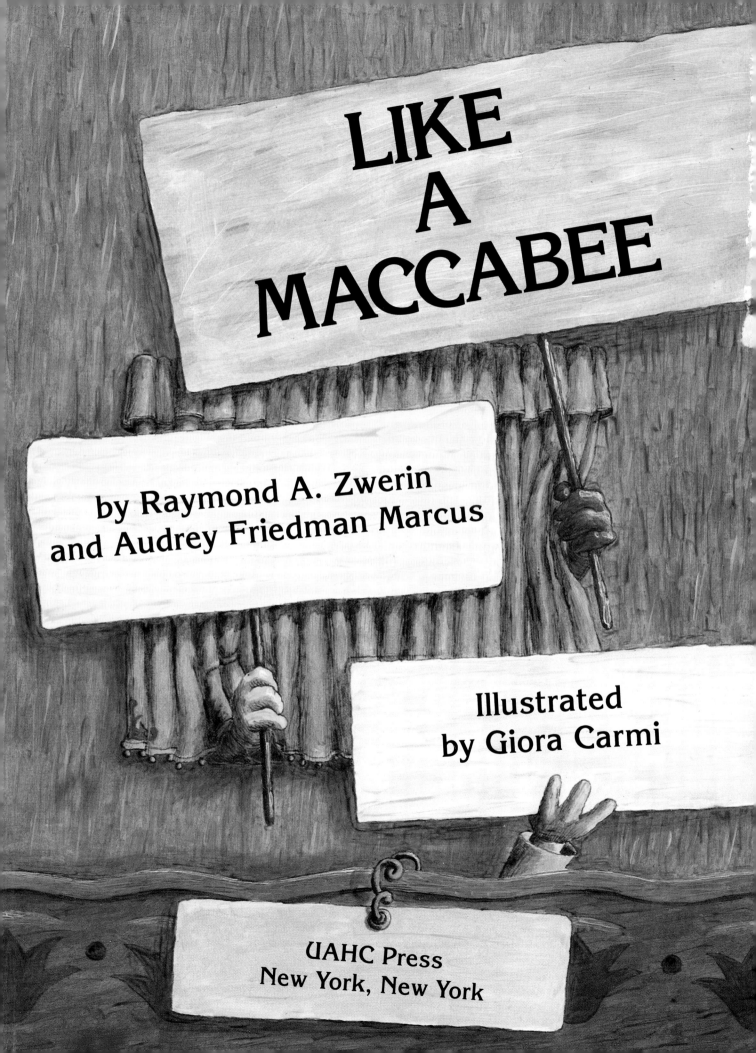

LIKE A MACCABEE

by Raymond A. Zwerin
and Audrey Friedman Marcus

Illustrated
by Giora Carmi

UAHC Press
New York, New York

Long ago in the Land of Israel the Jewish people lived in peace. They celebrated their holidays happily. They enjoyed their special foods. And they came from far and near to worship at the beautiful Temple in Jerusalem.

But then something happened. The king of Syria wanted to change the way the Jews lived. His name was Antiochus. He wanted the Jews to stop celebrating their holidays. He wanted them to eat forbidden foods. He wanted them to bow down to idols and worship Greek gods.

Antiochus sent his soldiers into
Israel. They came to the little
village of Modin. They set up idols
and told the Jews to bow down to
them. The people didn't know
what to do. Then one old man
named Mattathias stood up and
said, "We will not bow down to
your idols. Whoever is for Torah,
follow me." Mattathias and his five
sons became the leaders of the
people. They were known as the
Maccabees.

Being a Maccabee means doing what is right. The Maccabees knew that it was not right to bow down to idols.

Do you know what is right? If you do, you are like a Maccabee.

Being a Maccabee means being brave. Mattathias was brave. He would not do what the Syrian soldiers wanted.

Are you brave? If you are, you are like a Maccabee.

Being a Maccabee means being a leader. When no one else knew what to do, Mattathias became a leader. He showed the people what to do.

Are you a leader? If you are, you are like a Maccabee.

King Antiochus was very angry.
"The Jews must obey my orders,"
he declared. "My soldiers will
teach them a lesson." The king
sent his large army to attack
Israel. His soldiers marched
through small villages. They
marched into towns. They even
marched into the city of
Jerusalem.

There they entered the Holy Temple. They set up idols. They spilled out all the holy oil. The Temple was no longer a place where Jews could worship.

The oldest son of Mattathias was Judah. He called for war against the Syrians. Judah the Maccabee and his brothers led the fight with few weapons and few soldiers.

But the Jews were determined to win. They fought well, and they fought wisely. After three long years, they finally won.

Being a Maccabee means being determined. The Maccabees worked hard for what they wanted. The Maccabees never gave up.

Are you determined? If you are, you are like a Maccabee.

Being a Maccabee means thinking before doing. The Maccabees defeated a larger army by planning carefully before each battle.

Do you plan carefully? If you do, you are like a Maccabee.

Being a Maccabee means working together. A small group of Maccabees defeated Antiochus by working together.

Do you work together with others? If you do, you are like a Maccabee.

As soon as the war was over, the Maccabees led the people to the Temple in Jerusalem. When they entered, they saw what damage the Syrians had done. Holy vessels lay broken and scattered all around.

The Temple had to be cleaned before the Jews could worship there. Everyone worked hard to make the Temple beautiful again. With a little bit of oil they lit the *Ner Tamid,* the Eternal Light. People say that these few drops of oil burned for eight days. They called it a miracle. Everyone said prayers of thanks to God.

Being a Maccabee means helping to fix what's broken. The Maccabees helped fix the Temple.

Do you help fix what's broken? If you do, you are like a Maccabee.

Being a Maccabee means bringing light and happiness to others. The Maccabees brought the light and happiness back into the Temple.

Do you bring light and happiness to others? If you do, you are like a Maccabee.

Being a Maccabee means being thankful to God. The Maccabees were thankful for all of God's blessings.

Are you thankful for all of your blessings? If you are, you are like a Maccabee.

Each year we celebrate the holiday of Chanukah and remember the Maccabees. For eight nights beginning on the 25th of *Kislev* we say blessings. We light our *chanukiah*. We sing songs about the Maccabees. We eat special foods, and we play dreidel.

The Maccabees did what was right. They were brave. They were leaders. They were determined. They thought before they acted. They worked together. They helped fix what was broken. They brought light and happiness to this world. They were thankful to God.

Are you like a Maccabee?